关注常青藤，关注儿童成长！

The Adventures of Angus
安格斯奇遇记

［美］玛乔丽·弗莱克◎著

曾志嫒◎译

九州出版社
JIUZHOUPRESS

目 录
CONTENTS

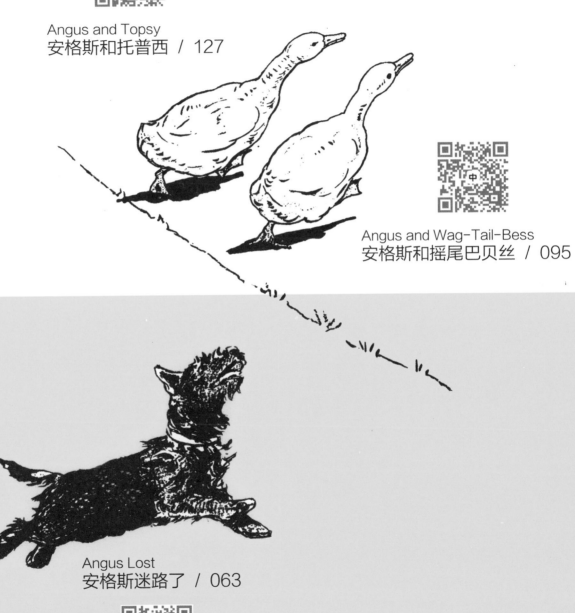

Angus and the Ducks
安格斯和鸭子

Once there was a very young little dog whose name was Angus, because his mother and his father came from Scotland.

Although the rest of Angus was quite small, his head was very large and so were his feet.

从前有一只小狗，名字叫作安格斯，他的爸爸和妈妈都来自苏格兰。

安格斯的个头儿很小，但头和脚却很大。

Angus was curious about many places and many things:

安格斯对很多地方和很多事物都充满了好奇：

He was curious about what lived under the sofa and in dark corners and who was the little dog in the mirror.

他好奇住在沙发底下和黑暗角落里的东西是什么，镜子里的小狗又是谁？

He was curious about things—which come apart and those things—which don't come apart; such as slippers and gentlemen's suspenders and things like that.

他还很好奇为什么有些东西能分开，而有些东西就分不开，比如拖鞋和男士背带裤等，诸如此类的东西。

Angus was also curious about things-outdoors but he could not find out much about them because of a leash.

安格斯还想知道门外的东西是什么，但他却无法去探索，因为他被一根皮绳拴住了。

The leash was fastened at one end to the collar around his neck and at the other end to somebody else.

那根皮绳的一端系着他脖子上戴的项圈，另一端被别人拽着。

But Angus was most curious of all about a noise which came from the other side of the large green hedge at the end of the garden.

但是最让安格斯感到好奇的，却是花园尽头那片高大的绿色篱笆墙外传来的吵闹声。

The noise usually sounded like this: Quack! Quack! Quackety! Quack!

But sometimes it sounded like this: Quackety! Quackety! Quackety! Quack!!

那声音通常听起来是这样的：嘎！嘎！嘎嘎！嘎！

但有时候听起来又是这样的：嘎嘎！嘎嘎！嘎嘎！嘎！！

One day the door between outdoors and indoors was left open by mistake; and out went Angus without the leash or somebody else.

终于有一天，屋外通向屋内的门被人不小心开着了，安格斯趁机溜了出去，既没有系皮绳，也没有人牵着他。

Down the little path he ran until he came to the large green hedge at the end of the garden.

He tried to go around it, but it was much too long. He tried to go over it, but it was much too high.

他沿着小径，一路小跑，一直来到了花园尽头那片高大的绿色篱笆墙边。

他试图绕过篱笆墙，但那篱笆墙实在太长了；他又试图跳过去，但那篱笆墙又太高了。

So Angus went under the large green hedge and came out on the other side. There, directly in front of him were two white ducks.

所以安格斯只好从高大的绿色篱笆墙的下面钻了过去。那里，映入他眼帘的是两只白色的鸭子。

They were marching forward, one-foot-up and one-foot-down. Quack! Quack! Quackety! Quack!

他们正朝着安格斯，高一脚低一脚地走过来。嘎！嘎！嘎嘎！嘎！

Angus said: Woo-oo-oof!!!

安格斯大叫道："呜——呜——汪！！！"

Away went the ducks all of a flutter.

Quackety! Quackety!

Quackety! Quackety!

Quackety!!!

鸭子们赶紧拍着翅膀跑开了。

嘎嘎！嘎嘎！

嘎嘎！嘎嘎！

嘎嘎！！！

Angus followed after.

Soon the ducks stopped by a stone watering trough under a mulberry tree.

Angus stopped, too.

安格斯紧追着他们不放。

很快，鸭子们在桑树下的一块石质水槽旁停了下来。

安格斯也停了下来。

Each duck dipped a yellow bill in the cool clear water. Angus watched.

Each duck took a long drink of the cool clear water. Still Angus watched. Each duck took another long drink of the cool clear water.

鸭子们将他们黄色的嘴伸进了清凉的水中。安格斯好奇地观察着。

鸭子们深深地吸了口那清凉的水。安格斯还在那里观察着他们。鸭子们又深深地吸了口清凉的水。

Then Angus said: Woo-oo-oof!!!
这下，安格斯抗议了："呜——呜——汪！！！"

Away the ducks scuttled and Angus lapped the cool
clear water.

鸭子们赶紧逃走了。安格斯过去舔了舔那清凉
的水。

Birds sang in the mulberry tree. The sun made patterns through the leaves over the grass.

鸟儿们在桑树上唱着歌儿；太阳透过树叶将影子洒在草地上。

The ducks talked together: Quack! Quack! Quack!

Then:

鸭子们凑在一块儿合计了一下："嘎！嘎！嘎！"

于是：

Hiss-s-s-s-s-s!!!

嘶——嘶——嘶！！！

Hiss-s-s-s-s-s!!!

嘶——嘶——嘶！！！

The first duck nipped Angus's tail!

Hiss-s-s-s-s-s!!!

第一只鸭子咬住了安格斯的尾巴！

嘶——嘶——嘶！！！

Hiss-s-s-s-s-s-s!!!

The second duck flapped his wings!

嘶——嘶——嘶！！！

第二只鸭子展开了他的翅膀！

Angus scrambled under the large green hedge,

安格斯急忙从那高大的绿色篱笆墙下面钻了回去，

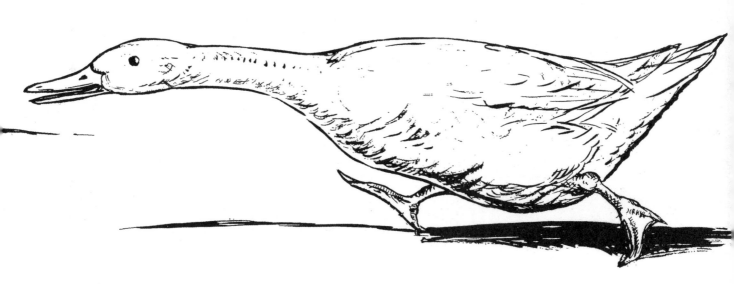

scurried up the little path,

匆匆地沿着小径，

scampered into the house,

迅速跑进屋里，

and crawled under the sofa.

躲到沙发底下。

For exactly three minutes by the clock, Angus was not curious about anything at all.

在接下来整整三分钟的时间里，安格斯对任何事都提不起兴趣来。

Angus and the Cat
安格斯和猫

Each day as Angus grew older he grew longer but not much higher. Scottie dogs grow that way.

Now as Angus grew older and longer he learned many things.

随着安格斯一天天长大，他的身体长长了不少，可是身高却没怎么增长。苏格兰犬都是那样长的。

现在，随着安格斯慢慢长大、长长，他渐渐懂得了很多东西。

He learned it is best to stay in one's own yard and frogs can jump but not to jump after them and

　　他知道：待在自家的院子里最好；青蛙会跳，但是不能跟着他们跳；

balloons go—

气球会——

POP!

砰！

Angus also learned not to lie on the sofa and not to take somebody else's food and things like that.

安格斯还知道诸如不能躺在沙发上，不能随便吃别人的食物等之类的事儿。

But there was something outdoors Angus was very curious about but had never learned about, and that was cats.

但是屋外的那些家伙真的让安格斯好奇不已，他从来都搞不懂他们，搞不懂那些——猫。

The leash was too short.

可惜绑在他脖子上的皮绳太短了。

Until one day what should Angus find indoors lying on the
sofa but a strange little cat!

Angus came closer—the cat sat up.

直至有一天，安格斯发现屋内的沙发上躺着一只陌生
的小猫。

安格斯凑近了一点儿——小猫坐起来了。

Angus came closer—up jumped the cat onto the arm of the sofa.

安格斯又凑近了一点儿——小猫一下子跳到了沙发扶手上。

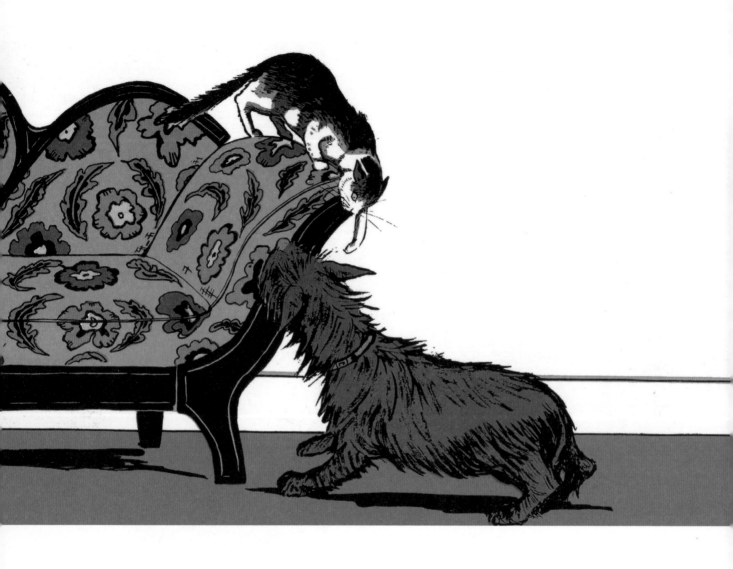

Angus came closer and—siss-s-s-s-s-s!!!
The little cat boxed Angus's ears!

安格斯又往前凑了凑。

嘶——嘶——嘶！！！

这下小猫使劲儿挠了一下安格斯的耳朵！

Woo-oo-oof-Woo-oo-oof! Said Angus.

Up jumped the cat onto the sofa back, up to the mantel—and Angus was not high enough to reach her!

"呜——呜——汪——呜——呜——汪！"安格斯愤怒了。

小猫赶紧跳回沙发，接着又跳到了壁炉架上——安格斯不够高，抓不着她。

But at lunch time down she came to try and take Angus's food—though not for long.

午饭时间到了，小猫从壁炉架上下来了，试着吃了些安格斯的食物——尽管没多久。

Up she jumped onto the table, and Angus was not high
enough to reach her!

接着，她又跳到了桌子上，安格斯不够高，还是抓不
着她。

At nap time there she was sitting in Angus's own special

午睡的时候，小猫占据了安格斯专属沐浴阳光的地

square of sunshine—washing her face,

方——洗她的脸。

though not for long up she jumped onto the window sill,

过了没多久，她又跳到了窗台上，

and Angus was not high enough to reach her!

安格斯不够高，依然抓不着她！

For three whole days Angus was very busy chasing that cat, but she always went up out of reach until on the fourth day he chased her up-the-stairs into the bedroom and she was completely gone!

　　整整三天，安格斯都忙于追逐那只猫，可是她总是跳
到安格斯够不着的地方，直到第四天，安格斯追着她进了
楼上的卧室里，彻底失去了她的踪影！

Angus looked under the bed—no cat was there.

安格斯看了看床底下——那里没有猫。

Angus looked out of the window into his yard,

安格斯又看向窗外自家的院子，

into the next yard—no cat could he see anywhere.

以及隔壁家的院子——他还是找不着那只猫。

Angus went down-the-stairs.

He looked on the sofa—no cat was there.

He looked on the mantel—no cat was there.

安格斯跑到楼下。

他看了看沙发上——那里没有猫。

他又看了看壁炉架上——那里也没有猫。

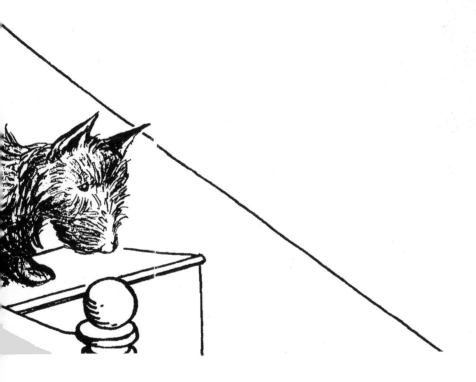

Angus looked on the table and on the window sills—no cat was indoors anywhere.

他还看了餐桌上、窗台上——可屋里什么地方都没有猫。

So Angus was all-alone. There was no cat to box his ears. There was no cat to take his food. There was no cat to sit in his sunshine. There was no cat to chase away. So Angus wad all-alone and he had nothing-to-do!

Angus missed the little cat.

这下安格斯感到孤独了。没有猫来挠他的耳朵，没有猫来抢他的食物，也没有猫来抢占他享受阳光浴的地方，更没有猫和他追逐着玩耍了。所以，安格斯觉得好孤独，无所事事。

安格斯很想那只小猫。

But—at lunch time he heard this noise:
PURRRRR—

直到——午饭的时候，他听到了这样的声音：

"喵——"

And there she was again.

And Angus knew and the cat knew that Angus knew that—

她回来了。

安格斯知道就是那只小猫———

Angus was glad the cat came back!

安格斯很高兴，小猫又回来了！

Angus Lost

安格斯迷路了

When winter came Angus grew tired of the same yard and the same house and the same cat and all the same things he knew all about.

Angus was curious about other places and other things such as—where the milk man came from and where the wide road went to and what kind of animals cars are and things like that.

冬天来临的时候，安格斯感到了厌倦：他厌倦了住在同一个院子和同一个房子里，厌倦了老是对着同一只猫咪，厌倦了那些一成不变的事物。

安格斯曾经对外面的世界和其他的事物都充满了好奇，比如说——送奶工是从哪儿来的，宽阔的马路通向哪儿，汽车又是一种什么动物，等等。

So one day Angus slipped through the gate and—there he was on the wide road.

于是，一天，安格斯偷偷地从门缝里溜了出去，来到了宽阔的马路上。

Angus looked up the road and he could see no end. Angus looked down the road and he could see no end.

安格斯抬头看向路的前面，但是他怎么也看不到尽头；他又低头看向路的后面，可他还是看不到尽头。

Then another dog came by.

"Woooof," said Angus.

"Grrrruf," called the other dog.

这时，一只狗从他身旁经过。

"汪——汪——汪。"安格斯打招呼道。

"呜——呜——呜。"那只狗也回叫道。

Angus and the other dog ran together up the wide road.
安格斯和那只狗一起跑到了宽阔的马路上。

Faster ran the other dog, faster ran Angus, but Angus's legs were too short.

那只狗越跑越快，安格斯也跟着越跑越快，但安格斯的腿太短了。

Faster ran the other dog, faster ran Angus, but—the other dog's legs were too long. Around the corner ran the other dog; around the corner ran Angus, but the other dog was gone.

　　那只狗跑得更快了，安格斯也跟着跑得越来越快，可是那只狗的腿实在太长了。那只狗跑到了一个拐弯的地方，安格斯也跟着跑了过去，但是那只狗突然不见了。

Instead there stood a stranger.

"Woooof," said Angus.

"Baa-aaaaa," said the goat.

"Woooof-woooof," said Angus.

　　站在那里的是一个陌生的家伙。

　　"汪——汪——汪。"安格斯叫道。

　　"咩——咩——咩。"山羊回叫道。

　　"汪——汪——汪，汪——汪——汪。"安格斯又
叫道。

But down went the head of the goat and its horns were coming
close, closer to Angus—

　　但这时那山羊低下了头，竖起了犄角，向着安格斯冲了过来，距离越来越近……

when the goat stopped, just in time!

还好，最后山羊停了下来，非常及时地停了下来！

But—zooom.

但是，“嗡——”

Came a car, coming at Angus!

一辆汽车朝着安格斯开过来了！

"Woooof," said Angus.

"Honk," said the car.

　　"汪——汪——汪。"安格斯叫了起来。

　　"滴——滴。"汽车也冲着他叫。

"Woooof," said Angus, and the car ran away.

"汪——汪——汪。"安格斯又叫道。

可是汽车开走了。

Then dark began to come and Angus saw two eyes looking
from a tree.

"Woooooooof," said Angus and—

夜幕降临了，安格斯看到树上有两只眼睛正盯着他看。

"汪——汪——汪。"安格斯叫起来。

"Whooo-whooo," called the eyes.

And Angus ran to find his house.

"喔——喔。"树上的眼睛也叫道。

安格斯跑开了，想找到回家的路。

But snow came, and wind came, and into a cave crawled
Angus,

　　可是，雪下了起来，风也刮了起来，安格斯只好躲进
了一个山洞里。

and he waited, waited and waited until—day came.

他等啊，等啊，一直等到了——天亮。

Rattle-rattle-clink-clink—

嘎——嘎——叮当——叮当……

there was the milk man.

送奶工来了。

Rattle-rattle-clink-clink-patter-patter.

嘎——嘎——叮当——叮当——嗒嗒——嗒嗒⋯⋯

Angus followed the milk man from door to door, from door to door until—at last Angus was home again!

安格斯跟着送奶工，从这一家到下一家，又从下一家
到另外一家，直到——最后，安格斯回到了自己的家！

Angus was glad to come back to the same yard and the same
house and

安格斯很高兴又回到了同一个院子和同一个房子，

the same cat and all the same things he knew all about.
又看到了那只猫咪和那些他熟悉的事物！

Angus and Wag-Tail-Bess
安格斯和摇尾巴贝丝

En

中

Once there was an Airedale puppy and she was named Wag-Tail-Bess because her mother's name was Bess and her father's name was Wags.

But Wag-Tail-Bess never wagged her tail or stuck up her ears or smiled as an Airedale should, so she was called plain Bess.

从前有一只艾尔谷犬，名字叫作摇尾巴贝丝，因为她妈妈的名字叫作贝丝，她爸爸的名字叫作摇斯。

但是摇尾巴贝丝从来不会像一只艾尔谷犬应该做的那样，摇摇她的尾巴、竖起她的耳朵或是露出一丝微笑，所以她又被叫作平庸的贝丝。

Bess was so shy she was afraid of almost everything, although she was big enough to know better.

When Bess was outdoors she was afraid to come indoors, and when she was indoors she was afraid to go outdoors.

贝丝非常害羞，几乎害怕所有的东西，尽管她现在已经大到可以去更好地了解事物了。

当贝丝在屋外时，她不敢走进屋内，而当她处于屋内时，她又不敢走到屋外。

When Bess was taken walking she was afraid to walk forward, so she would try to walk backwards, and when she couldn't go backwards—

当贝丝被牵着出去散步时，她不敢往前走，总是试图后退；实在退不了——

she would lie down.

她便赖在地上不走。

Bess was even afraid to eat her dinner.

She would sniff at it on this side and sniff at it on that side, until at last she would get so hungry. She would gulp down her dinner without chewing it at all.

贝丝甚至连吃饭都怕。

她总是这里闻闻，那里嗅嗅，直到最后她饿得前胸贴后背。这时，她就会狼吞虎咽地解决掉自己的晚餐。

Then Bess would be afraid because her tummy ached.

接下来，贝丝又会害怕起来，因为她的肚子开始疼了。

At night time Bess was afraid of a strange black creature. Sometimes it was small and sometimes it was large, but always it would stay with Bess wherever she went, crawling on the floor and climbing up the stairs and down the stairs, and sometimes on the wall.

　　到了晚上，贝丝还会怕一个奇怪的黑乎乎的家伙。

　　那家伙时而变小，时而变大，可无论贝丝走到哪里，它都会紧紧地跟着她——有时趴在地上，有时爬到楼梯上，有时甚至挂在墙上。

One day when Bess was outdoors, because she was afraid to go indoors, she heard these sounds come from the garden next door:

一天，害怕进到屋内的贝丝正在屋外玩儿，突然她听到隔壁花园传来一阵声音：

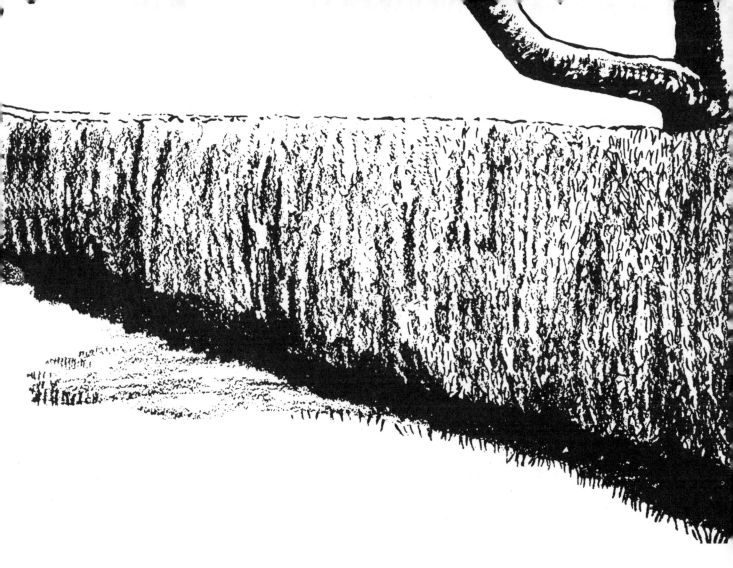

"Meowww!"
"Quack-quack!"
"Wooof-wooof!"
　　"喵！"
　　"嘎——嘎！"
　　"汪——汪！"

Then up in the tree came jumping a cat!

接着，树上跳上来一只猫！

Through the hedge came scuttling a duck,
从篱笆墙下钻出来一只鸭子，

then came another duck!

接着又一只！

And then came Angus!

很快，安格斯也钻了出来！

Bess was so surprised she forgot to be shy, so she also forgot to be afraid. So—Bess ran with Angus after the ducks!

　　贝丝好惊讶，甚至都忘记了害羞，忘记了害怕。所以，贝丝和安格斯一起追赶起鸭子来。

"Woooof-woof!" said Angus.

"Whoof-whooof!" said Bess.

"呜——汪——汪！"安格斯叫道。

"汪——呜——汪！"贝丝跟着叫道。

Around the garden they chased the ducks,

他们绕着花园追逐着鸭子，

down the path and through the gate, up the road and then in,

一路追过小径，穿过大门，又沿着马路，

the ducks ran to the garden where they belonged.
一直跑进了鸭子们自己的花园。

"Woooof!" said Angus and wagged his tail.

"Whooof!" said Bess, and she stuck up her ears and wriggled her middle and wriggled her back and wagged her tail!

That is how Angus taught Bess to forget to remember to be shy, and so Bess was never afraid of things any more.

"呜——汪！"安格斯摇着自己的尾巴叫道。

"呜——汪！"贝丝也叫起来，还竖起了耳朵，扭了下身体，晃了下后背，摇了摇尾巴！

就这样，安格斯教会了贝丝如何变得不再害羞，从此，贝丝对任何东西都不再感到害怕了。

Now every day Bess and Angus and the cat all play together and Bess is always called "Wag-Tail-Bess".

现在，贝丝每天都会和安格斯以及小猫一起玩耍。而贝丝也成为名副其实的"摇尾巴贝丝"了。

Because she sticks up her ears and wags her tail and smiles as an Airedale should.

因为她现在和其他艾尔谷犬一样，可以竖耳朵、摇尾巴和面露微笑了。

Angus and Topsy

安格斯和托普西

Once there was a little cocker spaniel puppy named Topsy, and all the home she had was a shop window. When Topsy was a baby puppy she had belonged to her mother, but now that she was older Topsy did not belong especially to anybody. So Topsy was very lonesome.

Every day Topsy would watch other dogs out walking with the people they belonged to, and every day Topsy would hope that somebody who needed a little dog would come into the shop and take her away to a real home to live in.

从前，有一只小猎犬，名字叫托普西，她的整个家就是商店的一个小橱窗。当托普西小的时候，她是妈妈的小可爱；而今她长大了，不再属于任何人了。于是，她感到十分孤独。

每天，托普西都会看到其他的狗和他们的主人一起出来散步，而每天，她也希望能有那么一个人会需要一只小狗做伴，然后来到店里把她带回真正的家。

One day Topsy saw a little girl and her mother walking by. Topsy heard the little girl say, "Look, mother, look at the sweet little dog!" Topsy barked and wagged her little tail, and the little girl said, "Please, mother, please buy me the sweet little dog!" but the mother said, "No, Judy," and they went away.

　　一天，托普西看到一个小女孩儿和她的母亲一起经过橱窗。她听到小女孩儿说："看，妈妈，看这只可爱的小狗！"托普西叫了一声，并摇了摇自己的小尾巴。接着小女孩儿又说道："妈妈，求你了，给我买下这只可爱的小狗吧！"但是小女孩儿的妈妈说道："不行，茱蒂。"接着她们离开了。

Every day after that Topsy would see the little girl named Judy go by the shop window with her mother, and every day after that Topsy would hear the little girl say, "Please, mother, please buy me the sweet little dog," and the mother always said, "No, Judy," and they would go away.

　　之后，托普西每天都会看到这个名叫茱蒂的小女孩儿和她的母亲从商店的橱窗前经过。而她每天都会听到小女孩儿和她的妈妈说："求你啦，妈妈，给我买下这只可爱的小狗吧！"而她的妈妈总是说："不行，茱蒂。"然后她们就离开了。

Then at last somebody did come into the shop and take Topsy away to a real home to live in.

But this somebody was not the little girl named Judy. This somebody was a little old lady named Miss Samantha Littlefield.

终于有一天，一个人走进了商店，把托普西带到一个真正的家。

她不是那个名叫茱蒂的女孩儿，而是一位叫萨曼莎·李特菲尔德女士的老太太。

Miss Samantha lived in a very large tidy house in the middle of a very large tidy garden, and Miss Samantha was very glad to have Topsy belong to her because she had no one else belonging to her such as children or grand-children or nephews or nieces or people like that.

萨曼莎女士住在一个宽敞又整洁的房子里，而这个房子位于一个非常大而又整洁的花园中。能够把托普西带回家做伴，萨曼莎女士非常开心，因为除了托普西之外，她没有其他孩子，比如孙子、外甥、外甥女等这样的家人。

Miss Samantha gave Topsy a new collar with Topsy written on it, and a new leash and a woolly blue sweater for cold days and some galoshes for wet days.

萨曼莎女士给托普西买了一条刻着"托普西"名字的新项圈儿和一条新的皮绳。天冷的时候，她会给托普西穿上一套全新的蓝色毛衣；而在雨天的时候，她还会给托普西戴上橡胶鞋套。

But Topsy hid her leash and tore her blue sweater and chewed her galoshes.

但是托普西把她的皮绳藏起来了，蓝色毛衣撕烂了，就连鞋套也嚼坏了。

Miss Samantha gave Topsy a large blue dish to eat out of, but when Topsy tried to eat her supper, Splash! Went Topsy's long ears into the dish, and out spattered her supper all over the floor and all over Topsy, so Miss Samantha tied up Topsy's ears.

萨曼莎女士给托普西拿来了一个蓝色大盘子用来进餐，但是当托普西想要吃饭的时候，"嘣"的一声，托普西的长耳朵掉进了汤汁里，使得晚饭一下子全溅到了地板上和托普西的身上。于是，萨曼莎女士把托普西的耳朵绑了起来。

Miss Samantha tied up Topsy's ears with a red ribbon, but then Topsy would not eat out of her new blue dish. Topsy liked the dust bin better.

萨曼莎女士用红色的缎带把托普西的耳朵绑起来，但是后来，托普西不想用新的蓝色盘子进餐，她反而更喜欢用垃圾桶来吃饭。

Miss Samantha gave Topsy a beautiful new bed with a green pillow to sleep on and a yellow blanker to sleep under,

　　萨曼莎女士还给托普西买了一张漂亮的新床，在上面放了一个绿色的枕头和黄色的毯子，这样托普西就可以躺在上面美美地睡觉了。

but Topsy liked Miss Samantha's bed better.
但是托普西更喜欢跑到萨曼莎女士的床上睡觉。

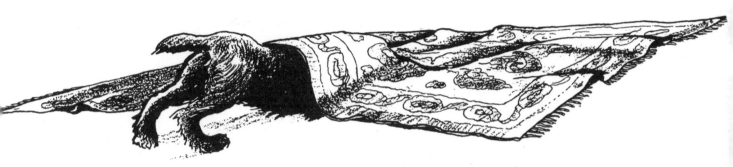

Miss Samantha gave Topsy a rubber bone to play with, but Topsy found a real bone instead. Topsy hid the real bone, hid it away in Miss Samantha's bed, and then Topsy found many things to play with.

Topsy found rugs to slide on and to crawl under.

萨曼莎女士给了托普西一根塑胶骨头玩耍，但是托普西却找来了一根真骨头。她把真骨头藏了起来，藏到萨曼莎女士的床底下，而且后来她又找来了更多的东西供自己玩耍。

她发现可以在地毯上面滑行，也可以在地毯下面爬行。

Topsy found feathers inside the sofa pillows, and Topsy found strange wire things inside the sofa, and soon Topsy found so many things to play with that Miss Samantha's large house was no longer tidy, and Miss Samantha was very sad.

Miss Samantha said, "Topsy, you are a very naughty little dog, you will have to live in the cellar."

140

　　她还发现沙发枕头里面的羽毛和沙发里面的一根根奇
奇怪怪的线可以玩儿，而很快，托普西又找到了更多好玩
儿的东西，而萨曼莎女士的家就再也不是从前那个整洁的
大房子了，这让萨曼莎女士感到非常懊恼。

　　萨曼莎女士对托普西说："托普西，你这只淘气的小
狗，我要把你送到地窖里面去住。"

So Topsy was very sad because she had to live in the cellar.

托普西觉得很伤心，因为她要住到地窖里去了。

But Topsy was not sad for long, because she climbed up the coal and out of a window and into the large tidy garden.

但是托普西并没有压抑许久，因为很快她便爬上了煤炭堆，爬出窗外，来到了一个宽大而又干净的花园里。

Topsy ran through tulips and over the pansies,

托普西穿过了郁金香，跃过了紫罗兰，

and under the back gate.

从花园的后门钻了出去。

And there was Angus.

"Yip-yip!" said Topsy.

"Woof-woof!" said Angus.

在那儿，她遇见了安格斯。

"汪——汪！"托普西问候道。

"呜——呜！"安格斯回应道。

So Angus and Topsy romped up and down and around the garden and under the hedge into the next garden.

接着，安格斯和托普西就在花园里追打嬉闹起来，还钻进树篱，来到隔壁家的花园。

And there was Wag-Tail-Bess!

So Angus and Topsy and Wag-Tail-Bess all romped up and down and around and around.

在那儿，他俩又看到了摇尾巴贝丝。

就这样，安格斯、托普西和贝丝三只狗一起在院子里上上下下、来来回回地嬉闹起来。

Then—plop—plop on the ground in front of Topsy bounced a red rubber ball!

"扑通——扑通！"一只红色的橡皮球弹着跳着来到了托普西的面前。

Topsy saw a little girl looking over the wall.

托普西还看到一个小女孩儿从围墙外看过来。

Topsy saw a little girl come running for her ball.

很快，小女孩儿跑过来，想要拿回自己的球。

And Topsy saw that this little girl was Judy!

"Yip-yip!" barked Topsy and wagged her little tail, and Judy said, "Why, it's my own little dog, my own little, sweet little dog who lived in the shop window!"

托普西认出这个小女孩儿就是茱蒂。

"汪——汪！"托普西叫着，摇着自己的小尾巴。而茱蒂也说道："这不是我的小狗吗？那只住在商店橱窗里面可爱的小狗！"

And Topsy licked Judy's red cheeks, and then Angus and Wag-Tail-Bess and Topsy and Judy all romped together until supper time.

　　然后，托普西舔了舔茱蒂那红红的小脸。接着，安格斯、摇尾巴贝丝和托普西，还有茱蒂一起在院子里跑跑跳跳地玩儿了起来，一直玩儿到晚饭时间。

Then Angus went home to his house, and Bess went home to her house, and when Judy went home to her house Topsy went with her. And Judy gave Topsy some supper out of a small yellow bowl so that Topsy's long ears fitted nicely over it, and Topsy ate all her supper very neatly.

安格斯和贝丝各自回了各自的家，而托普西就跟着茱蒂回了家。晚饭的时候，茱蒂给托普西端来了用黄色小碗盛着的晚饭，这样托普西的长耳朵就正好覆盖在了碗的外面，而托普西也把晚饭吃了个精光，而且把碗舔得干干净净。

When Judy went to bed she made a cosy little bed for Topsy close to her own big bed, and Topsy and Judy were very happy.

But—the next day, rap-rap came a knock on the door, and there was Miss Samantha Littlefield!

睡觉的时候，茱蒂在自己的大床旁边给托普西铺了一张既舒适又干净的小床，托普西和茱蒂很甜美地入睡了。

但是——第二天，"咚——咚！"一阵敲门声传来，萨曼莎女士来了。

"Oh, there is my naughty little Topsy!" said Miss Samantha,
and Judy began to cry, and Topsy was very sad.

　　"噢！我终于找到我的小托普西了！"萨曼莎女士说
道。茱蒂开始哭了起来，托普西也非常伤心。

Then Miss Samantha Littlefield asked very kindly, "Little girl, would you like to keep Topsy for your very own little dog?"

Judy asked her mother, "Please, mother, please may I keep Topsy to be my very own little dog always?"

And Judy's mother said, "Yes, Judy."

Then Judy said, "Thank you, Miss Littlefield, for giving Topsy to me, but won't you be lonesome without any Topsy?"

"Oh, no," said kind Miss Samantha Littlefield, "I will buy a nice pussy cat to come live with me."

接着，萨曼莎女士非常亲切地问道："小姑娘，你愿意把托普西留下来，作为自己的宠物吗？"

茱蒂去问了她的妈妈："拜托了，妈妈，我们可以收养托普西吗？"

"当然可以，茱蒂。"茱蒂的妈妈回答道。

于是，茱蒂说："谢谢您，李特菲尔德女士，谢谢您愿意把托普西给我，但是没有托普西，您不会感到寂寞吗？"

"噢，当然不会。"和蔼的李特菲尔德女士说道，"我会再买一只漂亮的小猫咪来和我同住。"

So always after that Topsy belonged to Judy, and Judy belonged to Topsy, and Angus and Wag-Tail-Bess and Judy and Topsy all romped together every day.

从那以后，托普西就是莱蒂的小狗了，而莱蒂就是托普西的主人了。安格斯和摇尾巴贝丝也可以和莱蒂、托普西每天都在院子里面一起玩耍了。

图书在版编目（CIP）数据

安格斯奇遇记 /（美）弗莱克著；曾志媛译. -- 北京：九州出版社，2016.3

ISBN 978-7-5108-4247-4

Ⅰ. ①安… Ⅱ. ①弗… ②曾… Ⅲ. ①儿童文学－图画故事－美国－现代 Ⅳ. ①I712.85

中国版本图书馆CIP数据核字（2016）第045158号

安格斯奇遇记

作　　者	［美］玛乔丽·弗莱克 著　曾志媛 译
出版发行	九州出版社
地　　址	北京市西城区阜外大街甲35号（100037）
发行电话	（010）68992190/3/5/6
网　　址	www.jiuzhoupress.com
电子信箱	jiuzhou@jiuzhoupress.com
印　　刷	天津市豪迈印务有限公司
开　　本	650毫米×990毫米 24开
印　　张	7
字　　数	20千字
版　　次	2016年4月第1版
印　　次	2016年4月第1次印刷
书　　号	ISBN 978-7-5108-4247-4
定　　价	35.00元